Published by
PEACHTREE PUBLISHERS
1700 Chattahoochee Avenue
Atlanta, Georgia 30318-2112

www.peachtree-online.com

Text © 2010 by Janet Lord
Illustrations © 2010 by Julie Paschkis

Art direction by Loraine M. Joyner
Illustrations painted with India ink and gouache on 100% rag
hot press archival watercolor paper.
Title typeset in Nick Curtis's StonyIsland; text typeset in
International Typeface Corporation's Korinna.

Printed and manufactured in December 2009 by Imago in Singapore
10 9 8 7 6 5 4 3 2 1

First Edition

Library of Congress Cataloging-in-Publication Data
Where is Catkin? / written by Janet Lord ; illustrated by Julie Paschkis.
    p. cm.
  Summary: Catkin jumps off Amy's lap to go for his daily hunt, and although he
hears many creatures in the yard, he cannot find them.
  ISBN 978-1-56145-523-2 / 1-56145-523-7
  [1. Cats—Fiction.] I. Paschkis, Julie, ill. II. Title.
  PZ7.L8774Wh 2010
  [E]—dc22
                          2009024517

Where Is Catkin?

Janet Lord

Illustrated by **Julie Paschkis**

PEACHTREE
ATLANTA

Dedicated to Amy,

of course

—J. L. and J. P.

Catkin jumps off Amy's lap and climbs over the wall.

It is time to hunt.

Catkin sneaks through the grass.
He sees something shiny and small.

Kerik-kerik. Kerik-kerik.

Catkin hops...

Cricket hops deep into the grass.

Where is Cricket?

Catkin creeps by the pond.
He sees something green and spotted.

Garrump. Garrump.

Catkin leaps…

Catkin tiptoes by the shed.
He spies a long tail.

Squeak! Squeak!

Catkin jumps...

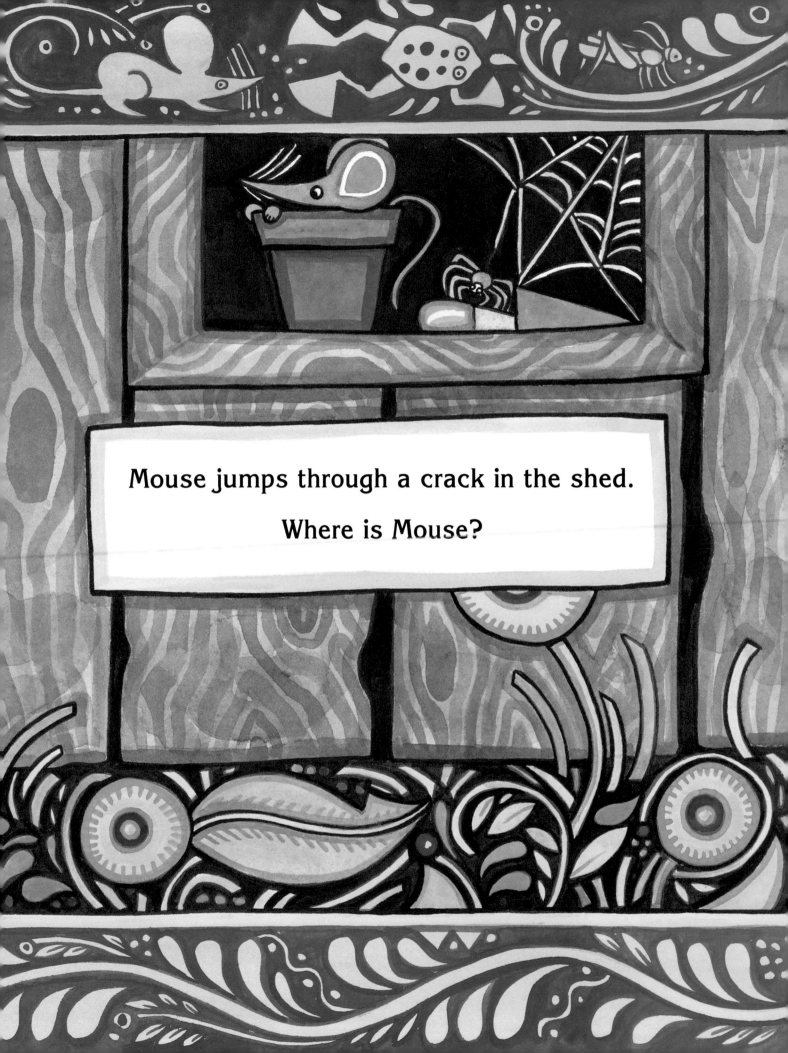

Mouse jumps through a crack in the shed.

Where is Mouse?

Catkin explores a rock pile.
He sees something long and striped.

Ssssssssssss. Ssssssssssss.

Catkin races...

Snake races between the rocks.

Where is Snake?

Catkin hears rustling by the tree.

Chereep. Chereep.

Catkin pounces...

Feathers fly.

Where is Bird?

Catkin looks around.
Everything is still.

Where is everyone?

Chereep. Chereep.

Catkin looks up.
His tail twitches
back and forth.
He digs in his claws
and climbs up, up, up
to the highest branch.

Catkin looks down.
It is a long way
to the ground.

Meeeoooow!

Amy stands up and listens.

Meeeow.

Where is Catkin?

Amy looks in the grassy field
and near the pond.

She looks under the shed
and between the rocks.

Meeeow.

Amy looks up
into the tree.

Where is Catkin?

Amy climbs from
branch to branch
to the very top.

Meeeow.

Oh, Catkin!

Purrrrrrrrr.